Lily and the
Christmas
Wish

KERIS
STAINTON

Piccadilly
PRESS

First published in Great Britain in 2015 by
Piccadilly Press
80-81 Wimpole St, London W1G 9RE
www.piccadillypress.co.uk

A CIP catalogue record for this book is
available from the British Library.

ISBN: 978–1–471–40512–9
also available as an ebook

1 3 5 7 9 10 8 6 4 2

Typeset in Sabon 14pt Extended by Palimpsest Book Production Limited,
Falkirk, Stirlingshire

Printed and bound by Clays Ltd, St Ives Plc

Piccadilly Press is an imprint of Bonnier Publishing Fiction,
a Bonnier Publishing company
www.bonnierpublishingfiction.co.uk
www.bonnierpublishing.co.uk

To Mum and Dad.

Wish you were here.

Also to Ellie Tiffin,

because you asked.

Chapter 1

Almost everyone Lily knew had gathered in the town hall. Her mum was sitting on her right, humming along with 'O Little Town of Bethlehem', and Lily's seven-year-old brother Jimmy sat next to Mum. Esme, Lily's best friend since preschool, was sitting on Lily's left, playing a game on her mum's iPhone.

Lily's dad was up on the balcony. He'd

peeped at her over the huge swags of green and red Christmas decorations to wave and pull a stupid face. Lily's mum had muttered something about his 'immaturity', but Lily had seen the corners of her mouth twitching, so she knew her mum thought it was funny really.

All Lily's teachers were there. Everyone from her school was there. Even Bobby, the town's only stray dog, was there (but Peggy from Knitwits was trying to shoo him out with a broom).

Basically, the rest of Pinewood was almost certainly empty. In fact, the only person Lily could think of who wasn't there was her grandad – and he didn't really leave the house any more.

At six p.m. precisely (Mayor Smith was

very big on punctuality) the carols stopped, the lights went down and the screen on the back wall lit up. Lily shuffled in her seat and leaned against her mum.

On the screen was an old map, showing Pinewood two hundred years ago when it actually *was* a pine wood. The map faded out to be replaced by a black and white photograph, but in that picture, the wood had disappeared. Instead the photograph showed the town square, the town hall they were currently sitting in, the shops and cafes that surrounded the square and the one lone pine tree standing proud in the centre.

Even though Lily knew exactly what the town she'd lived in her whole life looked like, seeing the change up there on the screen took her breath away.

The lights came back up and only then did Lily notice Mayor Smith standing underneath the screen, holding a wicker basket in both hands.

"Thank you all for coming this evening," she said. She didn't have a microphone; she didn't need one. She had one of those voices that projects. "I'm delighted with the turn out. I'm sure you're all aware that the bicentenary of Pinewood is approaching."

Lily certainly was aware. Her grandad hadn't talked about much else for a while now.

"Obviously," Mayor Smith continued, "we are going to have a celebration. But what? What could we possibly do to commemorate the two hundredth anniversary of founding such a wonderful place?"

"Fireworks!" someone shouted.

Lily looked around but she couldn't tell who it had been.

"Thank you," Mayor Smith said. "Fireworks would indeed be lovely, but it was actually a rhetorical question. What I meant was, what is the most important aspect of our town?"

"The people!" someone else shouted.

Lily looked up at her dad on the balcony. He winked at her.

"That was another rhetorical question," Mayor Smith said, wringing the basket in her hands. "But thank you again. I was actually thinking of the tree. The strong, proud pine tree that acts as a symbol of the strength and pride of the people of this town, and the centrepiece of our Christmas decorations."

"And as a toilet for Bug," Esme whispered, making Lily snort with laughter. She covered her mouth and turned it into a cough.

Dad had bought Bug the pug for Lily and Jimmy after he'd left last year. Their mum hadn't been impressed, but they'd all grown to love him. Although, actually, Lily hadn't had to grow to love him. She'd loved him from the first moment she saw him, wriggling in her dad's arms and making little grunting noises.

"So how do we celebrate the tree?" Mayor Smith continued, as Lily leaned down and scratched Bug behind the ears. And then, before someone could answer,

Mayor Smith rushed on. "We're going to turn it into a wish tree! A Christmas Wish Tree!"

She held the basket out in front of her and beamed. A low rumble of chatter ran around the room, but Mayor Smith cut it off. "In this basket are hundreds of paper luggage tags. I would like every single person in this town to take a luggage tag and write on it their deepest wish, and then tie that tag to the tree. Then, on Christmas Eve, at the traditional tree lighting ceremony, we'll take the tags down and add them to the town archive."

After a few seconds of silence, someone (Lily thought it was Hywel from the library) shouted out, "Who's going to make them come true?"

Mayor Smith's mouth turned down at the corners and the basket dropped to her knees. "Well . . . no one. It's symbolic."

"It's symbolic of not having a better idea of what to do for the bicentenary," Lily's mum said, as she, Lily and Jimmy walked back across the square towards their home.

"I liked what she said about the tree being a symbol of the strength and pride of the town . . ." Lily said. She bent down and picked up a crisp packet, before dropping it in the bin. "But what's the point if the wishes aren't going to come true? It'll just be like littering. But in a tree."

"Maybe it'll make people think about what they really want. What would make them happy," her mum said. "And then once they've thought about it, they might do something about it."

They reached the edge of the square and turned right, going past the *Pinewood Post*, the local newspaper where Lily and Jimmy's dad was editor.

"Do you know what you're going to wish for?" Lily asked her mum.

Her mum frowned. "I might wish that our house was a bit more . . . traditional."

Lily and Jimmy's mum and dad had bought the house when they got married. They'd thought it would be in good condition because they bought it off Toby Jones the builder, but it seemed Toby had used the house to try things out and experiment. That meant it was full of weird little problems, like the bathroom shower only working if the bathroom light was off (so they showered by candlelight), the 'self-washing' windows which never properly dried (so from inside the house it always looked like it was raining), and the doorbell that rang upstairs, but not down. They were mostly used to it by now, but sometimes it was a bit much.

"That's not very exciting," Lily said. "Wouldn't you want to wish to win the lottery? Or travel somewhere exotic?"

"Well, I always wanted to live in Paris." She looked wistful. "Before we had you and Jimmy, I mean. Me and your dad used to talk about it. We'd live in a tiny attic flat with big windows, views over the rooftops all the way to the Eiffel Tower. It

10

would be too hot in summer and too cold in winter, but it would be so romantic."

"Why didn't you ever do it?" Lily asked. Her mum's cheeks had gone pink and she had a funny expression on her face. Lily had never seen her look quite like that before.

Her mum shook her head and suddenly she was herself again. "Oh, it was just a mad dream. Your dad got his job at the paper and then we had you and we just forgot all about it, I suppose. We went for a weekend once, and we always said we'd go back, but we never did . . ."

"We could go," Lily said. "If we save up?"

Her mum smiled. "That would be nice." She put her hand in her pocket and pulled out a twenty-pence piece. "Will this do to start us off?"

"Can I wish for a funfair?" Jimmy said.

"I don't see why not," Lily's mum said. "What will you wish for, Lily?"

Lily looked over at the tree. It really did look proud and strong, its branches reaching out over at least half of the square.

"I don't know," she lied.

At home, Lily pinned the luggage tag to the noticeboard on her bedroom wall. It dangled between a photo of her and her dad when she was little, sitting on his shoulders at the beach, and a drawing of Bug Esme had done for her when they were bored in assembly.

The tag was just a plain brown piece of card attached to a short white string, but there was something about it that captured Lily's imagination. She pictured it tied to an old-fashioned luggage trunk, flapping in the breeze as the trunk was hoisted onto a ship destined for New York. Or the West Indies. Or Australia!

She pictured it fastened through the button-hole of a grubby-looking child being evacuated during World War II. They'd learned about evacuees at school and Lily still couldn't quite believe children were sent away without their families.

She pictured it tied to a balloon, flying high, high, high above Pinewood, buffeted by the wind.

"What do you think I should wish for?" she asked Bug, who was sitting down and dragging himself across her bedroom carpet with his front legs. He stopped and looked up at her, his dark eyes bulging and his pink tongue lolling out of his mouth.

"Why am I asking you?" Lily smiled. She bent down and kissed her dog on the top of his head. "I wonder what you'd wish for . . ."

Bug rolled on his back and lifted his four short legs in the air.

Giggling, Lily crouched down to rub his tummy and Bug wriggled in delight, making little grunting sounds.

"Unlimited tummy rubs?" Lily said. "Like you don't get that anyway!"

Lily's mum shouted from downstairs and Bug flipped over before struggling up to standing.

"Come on," Lily said, picking him up and tucking him under her arm.

As she passed the noticeboard, she touched the luggage tag quickly with her finger, and then closed her bedroom door behind her.

Chapter 2

Over the next few days the tree filled up with wishes; beige luggage labels peeked out between the shiny baubles and sparkling icicle lights. At first, Lily didn't see anyone tying their label to the tree. The early wishers must have been self-conscious and done it when no one was around, but as more and more wishes were added, people became more confident and now

Lily hardly ever passed the tree without seeing someone tying up their wish on the low-hanging branches.

Lily and Jimmy had spent most of Saturday morning sitting at the back of their mum's shop, Tea Cosies, with Bug. After their mum and dad had split up, their mum had rented a shop facing the square and turned it into a sort of gift-and-lovely-things shop, filled with silk flowers, brightly striped tea sets, ceramic sheep, old-fashioned hardback children's books and crocheted blankets. It wasn't at all busy and Lily knew her mum was worried about whether she'd be able to keep it open, but even so it was one of Lily's favourite places in Pinewood.

"I need to do a stocktake," Mum said, after Lily and Jimmy had rummaged through

17

a box of old (and slightly grimy) Christmas decorations. "Go and get some fresh air – take Bug for a walk."

"Can we go and see Dad?" Jimmy asked.

"Of course," Mum said. "But don't forget he might not be there. Just give me a ring if you go somewhere else."

Leaving the shop, they crossed over to the square and Jimmy headed straight for the tree to find a wish he hadn't already seen.

As Bug snuffled around the grass at the bottom of the trunk, Jimmy read out the wishes he could reach to Lily. "*I wish I could be on TV . . . I wish I could be invisible for a day . . . I wish I could pay all my bills* . . . What's this word?" he asked her, pointing at a label directly above his head.

"I told you to read them yourself," Lily said, looking over at the Our Daily Bread bakery, where she could just about make out Esme behind the counter with one of her mums. "I'm not interested."

Lily did find it hard to resist, though. There was something compelling about reading people's deepest dreams, even if you didn't know who that dream belonged to. But lots of the wishes were sad. More than Lily would have imagined. She hadn't realised how many people in this town had lost someone until she saw how many people were wishing loved ones could come back.

"Unlimited wishes! Unlimited wishes! Unlimited wishes!" Jimmy said, pointing at three more tags.

19

Lily laughed. "Fat chance! Come on, let's go and see Esme."

"Can I have a doughnut?"

Lily grabbed her brother's hand. "What do you think?"

"Fat chance?" he said and grinned.

"Have you made your wish yet?" Esme asked, before they were even inside the store.

Lily was trying to tie Bug to the pole outside, but he wasn't keen. The combination of baked goods and Esme was too much for him to resist.

"Will you stay there!" Lily said, trying to push his bottom down onto the pavement. "Be a good dog!"

"I've made my wish," Jimmy said, looking at Esme, shyly.

"Have you?" Lily asked him, surprised. "I didn't see you put a wish up."

"That's cos I did it when you weren't looking," he said. "Can I have a pink one?" He pointed at the pile of doughnuts behind the glass counter.

"You can have *two* pink ones," Esme said, grinning at him and putting her finger to her mouth to tell him to keep it quiet.

"No, he can't," Lily said, from the doorway, where Bug was now trying to wrap himself and his lead around her legs. "Mum says doughnuts send him daft. He shouldn't even have one really."

But Esme handed Jimmy a pink doughnut

wrapped in a napkin anyway, and he shoved it straight in his mouth.

"So what have you wished for?" Lily asked her brother.

"I'm not telling you," he said, doughnut crumbs flying everywhere.

Lily rolled her eyes. "What about you?" she asked Esme. "Have you done yours?"

Esme nodded. "And I'm not telling you either. If you tell people, they won't come true."

"They won't come true anyway!" Lily said. "That's not the point."

It was Esme's turn to roll her eyes. "You're no fun."

Jimmy giggled, spraying more doughnut crumbs, and Lily gave him a look.

"Have you got any Eccles cakes?" Lily asked. "We're going to Dad's."

"Hello, me hearties!" Jimmy shouted, as he and Lily approached their dad's canal boat.

"It's not a pirate ship," Lily said, rolling her eyes at her brother.

Their dad had bought *Fishful Thinking* when he and their mum had split up, after looking at a few flats and declaring them 'soul-destroying'. The boat had needed a bit of work doing, but now he had it almost as he wanted it, he said.

Their dad appeared at the open area at the back and perched on the yellow railing. He was wearing an ABBA T-shirt and a hat made from folded newspaper.

"I wasn't expecting you two!" he said,

grinning. "Not today." He frowned. "It is Saturday, isn't it?"

"Mum chucked us out of the shop," Lily told him. "She's stocktaking."

"Ah," Dad said. "It's important to know how many candles and heart-shaped rocks you've sold."

"I brought you some Eccles cakes but I don't think you should have them now," Lily said, pretending to be annoyed.

"I take it back!" her dad said, holding his hands up. "Your mum's shop is glorious and you are wonderful and I have missed you both!"

He reached out his hand to help Jimmy onto the boat and then Lily passed Bug over. Both Jimmy and Bug ran straight down the few steps to the inside of the cabin.

24

Suddenly feeling nervous, Lily shoved the box of Eccles cakes at her dad. He took off his newspaper hat and swept into a bow.

"Careful!" Lily said, as he straightened up.

He pretended to stagger, as if he was going to fall off the boat and Lily felt herself blush, which annoyed her. Since their dad had left home, Lily always found it took her a little bit of time to get used to him again, particularly when they saw him on his boat. The boat was fantastic and she loved it, but it was just so unusual. So Not Dad. Not Old Dad, anyway.

"Come and have a cake," Dad said, ducking his head to step down inside the boat. Lily followed him into the living area.

Inside the boat was all wood – the floor,

the walls, the ceiling. It was kind of like being in a tree house. In the middle of the room there was a small table bolted to the floor, and there was a corner sofa, piled with multi-coloured cushions. A tiny Christmas tree stood in a pot under the window. The star on the top needed straightening, but Lily could see the loo-roll Father Christmas decoration she'd made at preschool and it made her tummy feel funny.

Jimmy had already switched on the small wall-mounted TV, but Dad took the remote out of his hand, saying "No TV. I think we should go for a drive."

"You got a car?" Jimmy said, excited.

"No, remember?" Lily said. "You don't sail a canal boat, you drive it."

"That's right!" Dad said. "Because it doesn't have sails."

"Can I drive?" Jimmy said.

"I don't see why not!"

"I do," Lily muttered. "He's seven."

Her dad and Jimmy went back outside and Lily found the life jackets in the cupboard under the steps.

"Ah, it's a good job we've got someone responsible on board," Dad said, when she took them upstairs. Bug had jumped up on the sofa and fallen asleep, so at least she didn't need to worry about him. "Thanks for coming, Lils," her dad said, draping an arm around her shoulder.

It was the 'Lils' that did it – Lily felt herself relax and, once they'd pulled away from the mooring and were chugging down the canal, she let her head rest on her dad's shoulder. He still smelled exactly the same. That always surprised her for some reason.

They spent the rest of the afternoon on the canal and Lily loved it, even though it was so cold outside that they all had to snuggle together, wrapped in an old blanket that smelled a bit like the laundry basket. They saw geese and swans and about a dozen traffic cones (Jimmy tried to talk their dad into fishing one out for his room, but he had no luck).

By the time they got back to their dad's mooring, it was late afternoon. The sun was low and everything felt soft and sleepy. Jimmy *was* actually dozing on the sofa, and Lily, still sitting with her dad, kept having to force her eyes to stay open. She wanted to remember every detail. She hadn't had such a good time for ages.

"Is everything okay with you, Lils?" her dad asked quietly, before kissing her on the forehead.

Lily glanced at the winter sunshine sparkling on the water and then sheltered her eyes to look at her dad. "Fine, thank you. Yes."

"How's Bug doing?"

Lily looked down at him now – he'd come up on deck eventually and after barking at a few ducks, had fallen asleep on Lily's feet.

"He's great," Lily said.

"I hope he's not sleeping in your bed . . ." Dad said, in a tone that made it clear he knew he would be.

"Of course not." Lily giggled.

"I just want to know you're happy. I know things have been hard . . ."

"I'm fine," Lily said. The fluttery feeling was back in her stomach. She didn't want to talk about this. There had been so many of these talks before their parents had split up. In fact, one of the only good things about them finally splitting was that she didn't have to have any of these talks. She shuffled on the fold-up chair.

"Okay, okay," Dad said, holding his hands out. "I'll shut up. I just love you. That's all. Is that okay? You know that, right?"

"I know it," Lily said.

Chapter 3

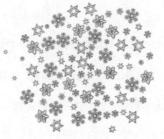

By the time Lily and Jimmy set off for home, the sky had turned a strange muddy-yellow colour. Heavy-looking white clouds seemed to be gathering directly above them, but in the gap between the clouds and the ground, a yellowish light was shining, as if they could see the actual rays of the sun.

"We'd better get a move on," Lily said, as they walked along the canal bank towards town. Something felt strange in the air too, Lily thought. It almost felt too thick, as if Lily was having to push her way through it.

They'd just clambered over the stile – Bug wriggling underneath and then turning back to wait for them – when snow started to fall.

"It's snowing!" Jimmy shouted, lifting his face up and sticking his tongue out to try to catch the flakes. "This is awesome!"

Lily wasn't so sure. Her skin felt crackly, like her clothes sometimes did when she took them out of the drier. She picked up Bug and cuddled him into her side.

By the time they reached the square, they were in the middle of a blizzard. The snow seemed to be coming at them from every direction – including straight into their faces – and the pavement was icy under their feet. Lily tugged Jimmy under the awning of the Coffee Cup Cafe.

"Maybe we should wait here until it stops," she said.

"I want to make snow angels!" Jimmy said, his bottom lip sticking out in disappointment.

"We can do that later," Lily said. "If it sticks."

Bug wiggled with excitement and licked the melting snow off Lily's neck.

The square seemed to be completely empty, although it was hard to tell through the snow. Lily could just about see the bright fairy lights strung between the streetlamps swinging in the wind. She really didn't want to be stuck there if the snow didn't stop. They should probably try to get at least a bit closer to home.

"I'll count to three and then we'll run – carefully! – to the next corner," Lily told Jimmy.

She took her brother's hand and, on the count of three, they started to run. They hadn't quite made it when a crack of thunder seemed to rattle every building on the square.

"I don't like it," Jimmy almost shouted.

Lily glanced at her brother, still tugging him towards the end of the street. His face was wet, his cheeks were pink and his eyes were suddenly wide with fear.

"It's fine," she said. "It's only thunder. It can't hurt us."

When they reached the corner, they sheltered in the doorway of the *Pinewood Post*, turning instinctively to look at the picture of their dad in the window. It said, *Giles Cooper, Editor* underneath and it was a really great picture of him – they used to have a framed version on the wall at home, when he still lived at home. He was smiling, his hair standing up in tufts, a grey scarf around his neck. Lily felt better just for seeing him there. It was only a storm.

More thunder rumbled, so loudly that Lily actually looked up, almost expecting to see the clouds crashing together. The clouds did seem lower and darker than before. In fact, Lily didn't think she could ever remember a sky like it. And was there usually thunder with a snow storm? She wasn't sure.

Suddenly a bright flash lit up the entire square. It was so bright it almost hurt Lily's eyes. She stepped backwards, bumping against the door of the newspaper office. She heard Jimmy scream and felt his arms around her waist.

"It's okay," she said, hugging him, his wet hair against her neck.

"I want to go home," Jimmy said. He sounded like he was about to cry.

"I do too," Lily said. "But I think we should probably wait here. You're not supposed to be out in the open when there's lightning."

Lily squeezed her brother and he snuggled into her side. With Bug under one arm and Jimmy under the other, she watched the snow swirling and wondered how long they'd be stuck there. It couldn't snow so heavily for very long, surely? Another crack of thunder made Jimmy jump and Bug whimper, but the next rumble was quieter and gentler than the last.

"There you go," Lily said. "It's going away now. We just need to wait a few minutes to make sure it's stopped and then we can go home."

But then the clouds cracked with thunder and Lily felt the hair stand up on her arms and the back of her neck. The sky lit up with a weird yellowish glow and then a fork of lightning zigzagged across the square.

Lily gasped.

Jimmy screamed.

Bug howled.

And the lightning hit the Christmas tree.

The snow stopped. Just stopped. One minute it had been coming down in flurries and then . . . nothing.

Lily put Bug down on the wet ground and hugged Jimmy. She could feel him trembling.

She squeezed him. "It's stopped. It's over. We're fine."

Bug barked and Lily picked him up again. She felt a bit shaky, so she wasn't surprised her dog was nervy too. He wriggled in her arms as if he was trying to snuggle inside her clothes. She nuzzled the back of his wrinkled neck, breathing in his familiar wet dog smell.

"Can we go home now?" Jimmy asked. He still had his eyes closed.

"Yes!" Lily said. "Open your eyes, you twit!"

Jimmy opened his eyes and Lily saw them widen, his mouth falling open. And when she looked over at the square, she saw why – the Christmas tree had been split completely in two.

Chapter 4

When they got home, they were greeted by their mum running out into the street and picking both of them up and squeezing them hard. She put Lily down (Jimmy stayed with his legs wrapped around his mum's waist like a chimp) and, as they walked up the front path into the house, Lily saw her grandad at the big front room window. He looked pale and scared, one hand pressed flat against the glass. Lily lifted her own hand to wave at him, but the sight of him standing there made her chest hurt.

Later, after they'd had a special 'We Survived the Storm' tea of crumpets with cheese (for the main course) and crumpets with jam (for pudding), and Jimmy had convinced them to watch his old preschool videos (the 'You've Got a Friend in Me' song always made them cry), followed by two chapters of *Matilda* curled up in their mum's bed drinking Grandad's Special Hot Chocolate (hot milk with Maltesers melted into it), Lily headed to her room to go to sleep.

She kicked off her slippers, dropped her dressing gown over the back of her chair and went straight over to the pinboard on her wall. The luggage tag on which she was supposed to have written her wish was still hanging there, still bare. She tapped its edge with her finger, making it swing gently from side to side.

"Oh well," Lily said, as Bug turned circles on the end of her bed. "Too late now."

Lily flopped down next to him and scratched him behind the ears.

"It wouldn't have come true anyway, eh, Bug?"

"You never know," Bug said and licked her hand.

Lily jumped in fright and stared at her dog, who was looking right back at her, eyes wide.

"What did you say?" she whispered.

She felt stupid even asking, because of

course he hadn't said anything. He couldn't say anything. He was a dog.

"I said 'you never know'," Bug repeated and rolled onto his back with his legs in the air.

Lily gasped. Bug's mouth hadn't moved. Or at least no more than usual – his tongue was sticking out and he was panting lightly – but his lips hadn't moved when he'd spoken, she was sure. She'd just heard the voice in her head . . .

But then she shook herself. Of course his lips hadn't moved. Because he hadn't spoken. Because he was a dog.

Maybe the lightning had hit her and she hadn't realised. Maybe it had done something to her brain.

Leaving Bug to wiggle in anticipation of a

tummy rub, Lily stood up and looked at herself in the small round mirror above her dressing table. She looked the same. Same heart-shaped face. Same bobbed hair. Same freckles. If she'd been struck by lightning, wouldn't her hair be standing on end and her face covered in soot or something? And, most importantly, wouldn't she be dead?

Lily saw the surprise on her own face in the mirror. Was she dead? Had she been struck by lightning, killed and now this was . . . Heaven?

She turned back to Bug. "Am I dead? Is this Heaven?"

"Don't be daft," Bug said. "You'd know if you were dead, wouldn't you?"

Lily knelt down next to her bed and put

her face as close to the dog's as she could and still be able to focus on him. "Well then, how are you talking?"

"I've always been able to talk," Bug said. "You've just never been able to hear me before."

It had taken Lily for ever to get to sleep. In fact, she had one of those nights when you would think you hadn't dropped off at all if you didn't know you'd had some weird dreams. Although none of her dreams were as weird as the fact that apparently she could now talk to animals.

Was it all animals or was it just Bug? That was one of the many questions that had kept her awake for much of the night. And apart from questions, there was just the general freakiness of saying in desperation, "WHY can't I sleep?!" and having a dog say, "Have you tried counting sheep?"

She wasn't sure what time it was. It was morning, but only just. She could see the pale yellow light starting to slide across the ceiling from the gap above the curtains. Bug was snoring next to her now, his funny little squashed-up face actually on her pillow.

Lily rolled on to her back, stretching her legs down the bed and wiggling her toes. Would her mum be able to hear Bug? Would Jimmy? Or was it just her? Had the lightning somehow made Bug able to communicate with humans? And why was she so convinced it was the lightning?

"It must've been!" she said out loud,

shuffling up the bed and leaning back on her padded headboard.

"Whaa?" Bug said, trying to flip over and failing, his bum wiggling in the air.

"Sorry," Lily said. "I was talking to myself."

"You do that a lot," Bug said. "I've noticed that."

Lily absent-mindedly scratched her dog's head and watched his eyes roll back with happiness.

"I do love you, Bug," she said.

"I know," said Bug. He butted her hip with his head. "I love you too."

Chapter 5

Lily carried Bug downstairs and sat him on the chair next to her at the dining table. He wasn't allowed on the chairs, but Lily felt like the usual rules probably shouldn't apply when your dog suddenly starts talking to you.

Jimmy was still in his pyjamas (navy blue with red rockets) and sporting his morning face and hair (face: scrunched. Hair: demented), but it was later than Lily had realised and their mum had already left for a meeting with her accountant. She'd be away from Pinewood all day.

Their grandad was trying to make coffee, but the machine was spluttering and ejecting coffee beans through a crack in the casing.

"Something weird's happened," Lily told Jimmy.

"Mmm?" Jimmy said, barely looking up from his console, which he wasn't supposed to have at the table. Or before school.

"Bug can talk," Lily said. She glanced over her shoulder to make sure Grandad wasn't listening, but he was rummaging in the messy drawer and muttering to himself.

Jimmy snorted. "No he can't."

"Jimmy," Lily said, doing her most serious voice. "He really can."

Jimmy looked at her and then said, "Go on then!" to Bug.

"What do you want me to say?" Bug said.

Jimmy's mouth dropped open.

"A-ha!" their grandad said at the same time, and pulled a roll of duct tape out of the drawer.

"How did you do that?" Jimmy asked Lily.

"It wasn't me," Lily said. "I'm telling you, Bug just started talking. Last night. Well, he said he's always been able to talk, we just haven't been able to hear him, but it's the same thing really."

Bug made a sceptical sound and tilted his head to the side.

"Say something else!" Jimmy said.

"You've got butter on your nose," Bug

said. "Want me to get that for you?" He hopped his front paws up on to the table and craned towards Jimmy's face, licking his own nose.

"Get down," Lily said.

Bug hopped down again, giving her a reproachful look.

"So . . . how?" Jimmy said, his game (and his breakfast) apparently forgotten.

"I don't know," Lily said. "I was worried it was just me, but since you can hear him too . . ."

"What's all this?" their grandad said, giving up on the coffee machine and coming to join them at the table. His thin hair was sticking up in tufts.

"Talking dog," Bug said, staring up at him and wagging his tail.

Grandad reached down and rubbed Bug's head, but didn't show any sign of having heard him speak.

"Huh," Bug said.

Lily raised her eyebrows at Jimmy.

"Nothing," she said to her grandad. "Did you manage to fix the coffee machine?"

"Nah," Grandad said. "I think it's beyond my skills." He looked over at it, frowning. "Packed lunches all done, though. Peanut butter for Lily and jam for Jimmy. That okay?"

"Yeah," Lily said, scratching Bug between the ears. "That's great."

After breakfast, and once Lily and Jimmy were washed and dressed in their school uniforms, they took Bug for a quick walk.

The street was bright with sunshine, but still a bit watery from the previous day's storm. While Bug sniffed around the trees, Jimmy hopped in and out of puddles and kept up a running commentary about how cool it would be now that Bug could talk. Bug ignored him.

They crossed the road, Lily holding Jimmy's hand, and Bug immediately darted after a squirrel, barking and giving half-hearted snarls.

"It's funny that he's still barking," Jimmy said. "Why isn't he shouting, 'Hey! Squirrel!'?"

"I don't know," Lily said. "Maybe the squirrel doesn't speak human?"

She looked up at the tree where the squirrel had darted as soon as Bug had started barking. The squirrel had stopped perfectly still against the tree trunk, but its bushy tail was twitching slightly.

Bug sat down, stared up the tree, and said, "We can still see you, you know."

Jimmy's shriek of laughter caused the squirrel to run along the nearest branch, which was too thin and bowed slightly under the squirrel's weight.

"What's that?" Lily asked, pointing up the tree.

"A stupid squirrel," Bug said, scratching his ear with his back leg.

"No," Lily said. "Near the squirrel. At the end of the branch."

She stood on tiptoes and, shielding her eyes against the morning sun, squinted at something that was hanging from a twig.

"It's one of the luggage tags," she said, eventually. "From the wish tree."

She looked around the base of the tree, grabbed a stick and started poking at the branch.

"If you could knock that squirrel down too . . ." Bug said.

"Shush," Lily said. Her tongue was poking out of the corner of her mouth and the tag seemed to be just out of reach, but then she managed to hook it and pull it down. The string snagged against the twig, snapping the twig and pulling a bit of the tag off with it, but the rest of the tag fluttered slowly down to the ground.

Lily stared at it for a second, with an uneasy feeling behind her knees, before picking it up off the floor and turning it over.

"What does it say?" Jimmy said.

The cardboard was damp and the ink was smudged, but Lily could still read the wish.

"It says, *I wish my dog could talk*."

Chapter 6

After school, Jimmy turned on the TV while Lily went straight up to her bedroom and tucked the luggage tag into her special tin. It was the tin where she kept all the things she didn't want to lose, like the hospital wristband from when she was born and the packet of forget-me-nots she was supposed to have planted after Grandma died, but had forgotten to.

She'd had the luggage tag in her pocket all day at school, and had touched it so much she'd been worried that she'd wear the writing off. Throughout the day, she'd heard people talking about some weird things that had happened since the storm, but nothing as big as a talking dog. And Bug was definitely still talking – he'd met her at the door when she came home to ask if he could have the crusts of her peanut butter sandwich (she never ate the crusts).

Now she looked at her own luggage tag, still blank and hanging from the pinboard. The others had probably been blown all over town by the storm, she realised. So they wouldn't be going in the town archive after all. Mayor Smith would be disappointed. Lily took the tag off and stared at the blank card, before grabbing a pen out of her drawer. There was no point making a wish now, she knew. But she wrote one anyway.

And then she frowned, scrumpled up the tag, and threw it in the bin.

When Lily got back downstairs, she found Jimmy and Grandad glued to the TV. Grandad was on the edge of the sofa, and Jimmy sat cross-legged on the floor with Bug curled up and snoring next to him.

"You have to watch this," Jimmy said, without turning round to look at Lily.

"What is it?" Lily asked, still standing in the doorway. But then she recognised what was on. It was the *Pinewood Post*'s community TV channel. Because so little usually happened in their town, the channel was a bit of a joke with most people. The presenter had once had to read aloud from a magazine she'd brought with her, because there had been just no news to report.

Lily stepped further into the room.

It wasn't Jolene Rose, the usual presenter on screen now. It was Myrtle Nutbeam, the cook from Lily and Jimmy's school. She looked completely frazzled. Her grey hair was bursting out of the bun she always wore on top of her head. Her bright pink lipstick was smeared on her teeth. There was something that looked like mustard down the front of her white snowman jumper. And she had a wild look in her eyes.

"Shush!" Lily said, even though no one had spoken. Not even Bug.

"We're getting reports of some . . . unusual events in Pinewood," Myrtle said, her voice wobbly.

Someone out of shot handed her more and more pieces of paper. They just kept on coming. And she kept looking more upset.

"Mrs Entwistle's cats have all disappeared," she read. "Melanie from the hairdresser's can't stop singing. Yaseen, the cameraman here, says that when he woke up this morning his fridge was full of cheese."

Myrtle took her glasses off and rubbed her face. "I can't do this any more! I don't know what's going on. I don't even know why I'm here on television!"

61

She stared into the camera for a few seconds while the papers kept piling up in front of her.

"I don't know what's going on and I don't like it!" she said. And then she burst into tears.

"I'm going to phone Dad," Lily said. "He'll know what's going on."

She went into the kitchen to get the phone and brought it back into the lounge, the long cord dragging behind her.

Her dad's mobile didn't even ring. Instead Lily heard the message, 'The mobile number you have called is currently unavailable. Please try again later'.

She told Grandad and Jimmy as she pressed the redial button, just in case.

"He's probably busy," Grandad said.

"He'll be looking into all this stuff for the newspaper." He'd taken a small notebook out of his pocket and was writing something down. "Do you remember what else Myrtle said?" he asked Jimmy.

"But he never turns his phone off," Lily said. "He leaves it on for work. And in case we need him. Can you try the office number?" She pressed redial again.

Her grandad took his mobile out of his pocket and held it at arm's length, squinting at the screen. Once he'd poked at the screen a few times, they heard an engaged tone.

So Lily tried her mum's mobile, but got an unavailable message from that one too.

"The one about the cheese!" Jimmy told Grandad, who nodded and wrote it down in his notebook.

63

"This doesn't make any sense," Lily said. She had a nervous feeling in her stomach. Like the back-of-the-knees feeling she'd had when she'd seen the luggage tag in the tree. Something definitely wasn't right.

"Grandad, can I go and see Dad at work?" she asked.

Her grandad looked up from his phone and frowned, shaking his head. "I don't think so, love. It's probably something and nothing, but I think we should all stay here until we know what's going on."

"I want to see Dad!" Jimmy said. His cheeks were pink and his bottom lip was quivering. He hated it when he couldn't get hold of their parents on the phone.

Lily pressed redial again. Nothing.

"We'll go straight there," Lily said. "I

promise. Straight there and straight home."

"You could come with us!" Jimmy said. "Then you wouldn't need to worry."

Lily noticed something that looked like fear cross Grandad's face, but then he recovered and seemed resigned.

"Straight there and back," he said. "No stopping."

As they headed around the edge of the square, with Jimmy walking with one foot on the pavement, one in the gutter, or leaping over bollards or swinging around postboxes, Lily looked out for anything else unusual. But everything looked pretty much the same. Peggy was using a hook on a long stick to pull down the awning outside Knitwits; Rayhan was setting out boxes of fruit outside the greengrocer's; Mrs Constantinou stood on a step-stool to water the hanging baskets outside Books Bizz.

Lily inhaled the scent of fresh bread from Esme's bakery and heard Christmas music coming out of one of the shops. From Myrtle Nutbeam's behaviour, Lily had half expected the town to be in chaos, but it didn't look like anything had changed at all. Except for the tree, which was mostly black with some bare wood right at the bottom of the trunk. The rest of the trunk had been split in two and curled to each side, like the pages of an open book. Lily thought there was a slight smell of burning, but maybe that was just her imagination.

The broken baubles and fairy lights had

obviously been swept up, although Lily could see a few colourful shards glinting in the grass. There was no sign of any of the luggage tags.

Before they had even opened the front door of the *Pinewood Post*, they could see that the newspaper office was really busy – even more than usual. Once Lily and Jimmy were through the door, they were hit by a wall of noise that sounded like every single member of staff (and quite a few people who didn't even work there) talking all at once.

Lily and Jimmy weaved between desks piled with papers, and squeezed past people tapping ferociously on keyboards, heading for their dad's glass-walled office. The closer they got, the more butterflies took flight in

Lily's stomach. She could already see into the office, and she couldn't see her dad.

"Tell him this is the worst possible day to be ill," shouted Fletch, the paper's deputy editor, when they were a few metres away. He had a pen in his mouth and another one behind his ear.

Lily blinked. "What?"

"Your dad. He's in a bad way, right? Must be at death's door to not turn up today." He picked up a phone and then put it down again. "I've been trying to ring him, but the phone lines are overloaded with all this . . . nonsense."

"What's wrong with him?" Lily asked, tugging Jimmy closer to Fletch's desk. The butterflies in her stomach felt more like birds, fluttering wildly and pecking at her insides. She felt Jimmy next to her, leaning against her slightly harder than was comfortable.

"I don't know," Fletch said. "Isn't that what you've come to tell me? That he's in hospital? Broken leg? Fractured skull? Contagious disease?"

"I don't know what you're talking about," Lily said. "How do you know he's ill?"

Fletch rubbed his face with both hands, then seemed to realise he'd made a massive assumption and frightened his boss's children.

"Sorry!" he said. "Sorry, Lily, Jimmy. I just thought he must be ill, cos he's not here and it's all kicking off."

He gestured around the room. His desk was covered with piles of paper, plain bits of paper with notes scrawled on them as well as newspapers. On the very edge was a pile of photographs that looked like they were about to slide off. Lily nudged them straight with one finger. The top photo was a black and white shot of Mrs Entwistle smiling and surrounded by cats. It was from last year's Summer Show. She'd won the Peerless Pet competition, mainly because she'd entered all fourteen of her cats and the only other entrant had been Barrington Cassidy's guinea pig, Bruce Wayne.

"So Daddy's not here?" Jimmy said.

Fletch shook his head. "You've tried the boat, right?"

"We'll go there now," Lily said.

"Well, if you find him, tell him to get his backside down here sharpish. We've had

70

more stories in the past half hour than the rest of the year put together."

Lily could believe that. In the bathroom on the boat, her dad had a framed front page that read *Shed Gone*.

Pulling Jimmy with her, she started to leave, but then stopped and turned back to Fletch. He'd picked the phone back up again and was staring at it with a puzzled expression.

"Fletch?" she said.

He looked up, his eyebrows making an upside-down V.

"What's happening?"

He shook his head. "I have absolutely no idea."

As Lily and Jimmy passed the cashpoint on the road that led down to the canal, they heard a woman muttering to herself about how she had more money than she should do in her account and wondering where it had come from.

"Maybe it's a computer problem," Lily said.

She'd heard both her parents talk about how when computers went wrong, everything could go wrong.

"Daddy will know," Jimmy said confidently, as they turned into Aspen Avenue and headed for the canal. "Like when Dad couldn't get money that time and Mum was really angry. And I didn't know why because it wasn't his fault, it was the bank's."

Lily frowned. She'd suspected that it wasn't so much that Dad couldn't get his money, but that there wasn't any money to get, but she didn't want to tell Jimmy that. Poor Dad. Living on a boat was expensive.

At the end of Aspen Avenue, they climbed over the stile to the canal path and walked the short distance to the bridge, where the canal curved slightly. Once they were under the bridge, they'd be able to see their dad's boat and usually their dad, sitting on the flat roof, reading a book.

Except today there was no Dad. And no boat.

Lily stared at the space where the boat should be. The fluttering feeling in her stomach was back.

"Has he moved?" Jimmy said.

"I don't know," Lily replied. "He didn't

say he was going to move, did he?"

She felt sick. Fletch hadn't been able to get hold of him and now this. Where was he?

"Maybe he's gone to the shops or something?" Jimmy said.

"Maybe." Lily frowned, trying to remember if their dad had said anything about going away. She didn't think he had. She was sure he hadn't.

"We can phone him again when we get back," Jimmy said.

Lily nodded.

As they walked back along the canal, Lily chewed on a loose bit of skin on her bottom lip. Maybe their dad had gone away and forgotten to tell them. But then he must've forgotten to tell work too and that wasn't like him. She frowned. He wasn't the most responsible father, that was true, but Lily couldn't imagine that he'd ever go anywhere without telling them. And he never let them down. Hardly ever.

Chapter 7

No one had been able to get hold of Lily and Jimmy's dad, or their mum. Every time they tried to make a call they got an 'unavailable' message. So when Mum got home from her appointment, she was surprised when Lily and Jimmy threw themselves at her, both talking at once.

"It'll just be a misunderstanding," she

told them, while Grandad kept one eye on *Pinewood Post* TV in case of any other odd events. "Your dad probably arranged to go away and forgot to tell us."

"But what about Fletch? He'd tell Fletch, wouldn't he?" Lily said.

"Not necessarily," her mum said. "Or maybe Fletch forgot. You said it was incredibly busy in the office."

"It was crazy," Lily said. "Something really weird is going on."

Her mum shook her head. "There'll be an explanation for all of it, I'm sure," she said. "Now I'm tired and grimy from the train. I'm going to have a bath and an early night, if that's okay with all of you?"

Everyone nodded. They knew she was

never in the best of moods when she'd been to see her accountant.

Once tea had been cleared away, Grandad read to Lily and Jimmy from *Swallows and Amazons*, which had been his favourite book growing up, and then they'd all gone to bed. Lily had planned to read her own favourite book for a while (*Malory Towers*), but she must have dozed off because she was suddenly woken up by a banging noise coming from downstairs.

Her heart pounding, she looked at Bug, who was standing at the end of the bed, his curly tail upright and his flat nose pointed at the door.

"Don't bark," she said. "What is it?"

Bug let out a low growl and Lily shushed

him. Both of them cocked their heads to one side to listen for the sound again. Three more bangs.

"It must just be someone at the door," Lily said, swinging her legs out of bed.

"Are they trying to break it down?" Bug said, jumping off the bed and trotting over to wait at Lily's bedroom door.

Lily went over to her window, which looked out over the street, but she couldn't see anyone on the path. She spotted headlights sliding away towards the square and wondered if someone had knocked and then driven off.

"What time is it?" she said.

"I can't tell the time," Bug said, scratching lightly at the door. "I'm a dog."

"Oh yeah. Sorry."

Crossing back to her bed, Lily pulled her bedside clock out of her top drawer (its ticking annoyed her) and found it was 9.15 p.m. It seemed much later, somehow.

"It's not that late," she said. "Maybe it's Dad."

She opened her bedroom door and Bug followed her out on to the landing.

"Mum!" she whispered outside the bathroom door.

"I'm in the bath," her mum called back. "Is someone here?"

"I think so . . ."

"Don't open the door," her mum said. "Not at this time of night."

"Okay," Lily whispered back, but she was already heading down the stairs. She knew that her grandad would most likely already be asleep or, if not, he'd have his headphones on, listening to Radio 4.

"Er, she said don't open it," Bug reminded her, hopping down the stairs at Lily's side.

"I'm not going to," Lily replied. "I'm just going to look. What if it is Dad? I can't leave him standing there."

At the bottom of the stairs, Lily pressed her face up against the pebbled window to the side of the front door. Whoever was there seemed to be wearing something bright purple. Not her dad, then. She squinted, but it didn't really help. She had no idea who it could be. She couldn't think of anyone in Pinewood prone to wearing bright purple.

"Lily, darling, is that you?" a voice called.

"Who's that?" Bug asked Lily.

81

"Grandmother," Lily whispered. Her other grandmother. The one who was still alive. Her dad's mum.

Lily tried to look through the window again, but only succeeded in hitting her forehead on the glass.

"Let me in, darling," she heard her grandmother say. "It's late, I'm old and your bell doesn't seem to be working."

"Hang on a minute," Lily said, rubbing her forehead. "I'll just get the keys."

The keys weren't in the door, so Lily went into the kitchen and retrieved them from the drawer under the spice rack. It always made her feel a bit ill getting them from there, since her parents had argued about it a lot.

Her mum said they needed to be away

from the front door because she'd heard of burglars reaching through the letterbox with a coat hanger, hooking the keys, using them to open the door and then robbing the house. Her dad argued that keeping the keys so far away from a locked door was a fire hazard. If ever Lily's dad went to the front door and found it locked, he'd stand there waving his arms and calling, "I'm burning! Burning! Avenge my fiery death!" Lily's mum hadn't found it the least bit funny.

Once she had the keys, Lily opened the door and took a step backwards at the sight of her grandmother.

What Lily had assumed to be a purple coat was actually a purple trouser suit, set off with a little round hat and knee-high boots.

"Hello, darling!" Grandmother said. "I

thought I was going to have to stay out here all night. You look delightful. Those pyjamas are adorable. Are you going to let me in?"

"Wow," Bug breathed, scrabbling backwards on the wooden floor.

Lily shushed him before remembering that she was the only one who would hear him.

"Did your dog just speak?" Lily's grandmother said.

Chapter 8

"You do know this has happened before?" Grandmother said.

They were sitting in the dining room. After Lily had gone upstairs, knocked on the bathroom door, and told her mum that Grandmother was there, Lily had heard water sloshing over the side of the bath and then smelled the whiff of candles being blown out. She'd waited outside the door, wondering what her mum was doing in there in the dark.

And then her mum had come out of the bathroom, her wet hair piled on top of her head and held up with what looked like chopsticks, a towel wrapped around her and a wild look in her eyes.

And after her mum had got dressed, they'd gone downstairs to find that the water that had sloshed out of the bath was dripping through into the living room, while Grandmother and Jimmy sat and watched it making a puddle on the floor. Then Lily's mum had gone to get a pan to catch the water, turn off the electricity at the mains and light candles in the dining room.

So after all of that, there they were, facing

each other in the flickering light. Silent but wide-eyed, directly opposite the grandmother they barely knew.

Grandmother took off her hat (she'd called it a 'cloche') and coat. Underneath, she was wearing a long-sleeved black shirt dotted with sparkly stones that looked like diamonds.

"She looks like a witch," Jimmy whispered to Lily.

"I'm not a witch, I assure you," Grandmother said. "And you really need to work on your manners, James."

Jimmy's cheeks flared red.

"What do you mean it's happened before?" Lily's mum asked her mother-in-law. "What has? When? And why are you here?"

"Pick one question and stick with it, Louise, darling," Grandmother said, before sighing. "The dog is talking. My son is missing. The town is in utter chaos."

"What do you mean it's happened before?" Lily's mum asked again.

"When?" Lily breathed.

"At the last centenary," her grandmother said.

"You were there?" Jimmy asked, and then clapped one hand over his mouth.

"Of course I wasn't there!" Grandmother said, rolling her eyes. "How old do you think I am, darling? No, I heard stories as I grew up. Wishes came true, but not for the people who made them."

"But how can it be possible?" Lily's mum asked now. "Wishes can't come true. They just can't!"

Lily's grandmother waved her hands in

front of her face and Lily noticed Jimmy's eyes widen. She knew he thought his grandmother was about to do magic.

"Wishes come true all the time, Louise. You've never wished for anything and had it come true? Really?"

"Well, yes, of course," their mum said. "But that's not because of the wish. That's just coincidence."

"How can you possibly know that?"

Lily's mum looked exasperated. "It's just common sense! Wishes can't come true. It's ridiculous!"

"What a shame," Lily's grandmother said and gave Mum a pitying look.

Lily looked from one to the other. Her mum thought wishes were just coincidences and maybe they were. But what if she was wrong? And her grandmother could hear Bug talking so maybe she was right. (Bug had been completely spooked by the revelation she could hear him too, and was currently hiding in the cupboard under the stairs, gnawing on the handle of the metal detector Jimmy had got last Christmas and had lost interest in by Boxing Day.)

Her mum said that wishes couldn't come true, but Lily knew they could – it had happened to her once.

"You think Dad's missing because of the wishes?" Lily asked her grandmother.

"It seems to be the most likely explanation," Grandmother said. "Don't you think?"

"I really don't," Lily's mum said.

"So what happened?" Lily said, frowning.

"Last time, I mean. How was it fixed?"

"I'm not entirely sure," Grandmother said. "My grandmother kept a book about it, but it's been misplaced over the years. If I remember correctly, it was something to do with the wishes being matched to the people who had made them."

"But how?" Lily said.

Grandmother brushed her hand back over her hair. "Well, Lily," she said. "I think that's probably up to you. If you're willing to try, that is."

Chapter 9

In the morning, Lily and Jimmy headed downstairs for breakfast together and then stopped dead in the kitchen doorway.

The dining table, which had been against the wall, under the serving hatch, was now in the middle of the room with chairs all around it (they'd only ever used four chairs since their dad had left).

In the space where the table had been

was a cupboard Lily had never seen before. It was low and long with doors on the front. Most of it was brown wood like the table, but the doors were painted with bright ice-cream colours. On top of it was a cream plastic church with brightly coloured stained glass windows. It seemed to be playing a tinny version of 'Silent Night'.

"I think maybe she *is* a witch," Bug said.

"I'm not," Lily's grandmother said from the table, where she was sitting with a large cup of coffee steaming in front of her.

"Huh," Bug said. "Forgot she could hear me too."

"I just thought the house needed a bit of sprucing up," Lily's grandmother said.

"What have you done?!"

Lily winced as she heard her mum's voice from behind her.

"Good morning, Louise!" Grandmother said brightly. "Just a bit of tidying."

"You've taken the doors off my cupboards!" Lily's mum said.

Oh yes. Lily hadn't even noticed that, but her mum was right. The wall cupboards in the kitchen were now open and her grandmother had obviously rearranged them, because instead of the usual cram of biscuits, bags of sugar, bags of pasta, boxes of teabags and tins of beans, there were piles of white dishes and pretty patterned glasses.

"Oh come in all of you, for goodness' sake!" Grandmother said.

"This is my house," Lily's mum mumbled as they all sat down.

Lily watched her grandmother as she dished up pancakes. She was wearing wide-legged velvet trousers and little patterned slippers with a soft, fluffy looking jumper and an apron on top. Her hair was up and she was wearing make-up, even lipstick. Lily couldn't imagine what time she must have got up to do all this. Maybe she never even went to bed.

"Can I smell coffee?" Grandad said, as he came through from the living room. "Leticia! I didn't know you were here!"

Grandmother turned and beamed at him. "I blew in on the evening wind," she said. "Pancake, Alan?"

"Please," Grandad said. "And coffee." He crossed the kitchen to the coffee maker. "I couldn't get the blasted machine to work, but it looks like you've got everything under control."

Lily saw her mum roll her eyes and then duck her head to try to hide it.

Once Lily and Jimmy had some pancakes and milk, and their mum and grandad had some pancakes and coffee, they all agreed (their mum a bit reluctantly) that it was the best breakfast they'd had for quite some time.

"So do you have a plan?" Grandmother asked Lily. "To find the wishes?"

"Oh please," Lily's mum said.

Grandmother ignored her.

"Grandad's got a plan," Jimmy said, collecting the last smears of syrup from his plate with his finger.

"Have I?" Grandad asked.

"You wrote the wishes down," Jimmy said. "In your notebook."

"Oh yes. The wishes Myrtle mentioned on TV," Grandad said, pulling a small hardback black notebook out of the pocket of his dressing gown. "I did. I wouldn't call it a plan, though."

"Can I see?" Grandmother asked.

Grandad pushed the notebook across the table to her and she studied it, running one elegant finger along the edge of the page.

"This is a good start," she said. "So what you need to do, Lily and Jimmy, is find the wish tags. And then find the people who made these wishes and put them together again."

"Oh is that all?" Bug said, from under the table, where he was eating the bits of pancake Jimmy had dropped.

"And if we hear of any more wishes happening, Alan can keep track of them," Grandmother said. "Oh and one more thing. I assume there was to be a ceremony? For the wishes?"

Lily nodded. "Christmas Eve. The tree-lighting. They were going to put the wish tags in the town archive. But they can't do it now, can they? Because there's no tree to light."

"I wouldn't count on it," Grandmother said. "But I would try to match the wishes before Christmas Eve. I'm not sure it will work after that."

"So we've got . . ." Lily screwed up her face to think. "Three weeks?"

"Plenty of time," Grandmother said.

But Lily wasn't so sure.

Chapter 10

"I think she's making it all up!" Lily said, grabbing Jimmy's arm to stop him stepping into the road.

"I like her," Jimmy said.

"I like her too," Lily said. "I think . . . But she doesn't have the book that talks about when it happened before, she doesn't remember the details of how they put things right then, but she also thinks we have to match the wishes and do it by Christmas Eve. How does she know?"

"But," Jimmy said, "what if she's right?"

Lily tugged him across the zebra crossing towards their school. "Yeah, I know," she said. "That's what I keep thinking. We have to try anyway, don't we?"

"Hey!" Lily heard from behind her. She stopped and waited for Esme to catch them up. While they walked the rest of the way to school together, Lily told Esme about her grandmother's theory about the wishes.

"It's mad, I know," Lily said.

"Yeah . . ." Esme said, pushing her pink crocheted beanie back from her forehead. "But there's obviously something funny going on. The tree in the courtyard behind our house has, like, doubled in size."

"Really?" Lily said. "Who would wish for a tree to get bigger?"

"No idea," Esme said. "I wished we could go to Disneyland." She clapped her hand over her mouth. "I wasn't meant to tell!"

"Do you know anyone who would've wished their dog could talk?" Lily asked. "That's a wish tag I found on a tree opposite our house."

"Lexi Spencer!" Esme said immediately.

"Really?" Lily asked.

Esme nodded. "She's always on about it. She wrote a story about it for Miss Buttons. She said her dog was her best friend and she told her all her secrets and she wished she could tell her hers. Something like that."

"I'll start with Lexi, then," Lily said.

But Lexi wasn't in school. Lily went to see the school secretary who said Lexi was off ill. "But she's not really ill," she said. "Her mum said she just can't come in. Something to do with the . . . you know." She pointed at the front page of the *Pinewood Post* on her desk. The headline was, *Be Careful What You Wish For*.

"So what will we do?" Jimmy asked Lily.

"I think we should go to her house. After school."

Lexi Spencer lived in a tiny terraced cottage in one of the yards off the main square. The gardens opposite the row of houses were glittering with frost, and dotted with painted chimney pots and brightly-coloured garden gnomes.

"I've never understood the point of these things," Bug said, before cocking his leg against one. After school, Lily and Jimmy had gone home to collect Bug because with Mum out all day and Grandad in all day, they knew he wouldn't have had a walk.

"Where are we?" Jimmy said, his eyes wide.

"Haven't you been here before?" Lily asked him. She'd been to a party at Lexi's house in Year 3. She hoped she still lived in the same one.

"It's beautiful," Jimmy said. "Hey, have you got the wish?"

Lily smiled. "The tag, you mean?" She took it out of her pocket and dangled it from her finger by the white string. She'd collected it at the same time as they'd collected Bug.

"*I wish my dog could talk*," Lily read.

"Will Bug stop talking?" Jimmy asked. "If you give Lexi her wish back?"

Lily opened her mouth and closed it again. "I hadn't thought of that. I hope not." She looked down at Bug who was standing nose-to-nose with another garden gnome and growling.

"Don't ask me," Bug said, without looking up. "I don't know how this stuff works."

"Maybe we should do a different wish first," Jimmy said. "And see what happens."

"We haven't got a different wish, though,"

Lily said. "So it has to be this one."

"Okay. But I hope he doesn't stop talking," Jimmy said. "He's funny."

Lily's tummy fluttered at the thought of Bug lying next to her in bed the previous night, talking about all of the squirrels he'd chased, to help her get to sleep.

"Me too," Lily said.

"Me three," Bug said, butting his head against Lily's leg.

"No talking in there, okay?" Lily said, picking Bug up. "I don't want to freak Lexi out."

"My lips are zipped," Bug said. Lily kissed him on top of his head before reaching up to knock on Lexi's door with the brass lion's-head door knocker. She half-hoped no one would be in, but she

106

heard someone sing, "*Just a minute!*" from inside, and then the top half of the door opened.

"Cool!" Jimmy said.

"Hey!" Lexi's mum said. And then she started to sing. "*Lily and Jimmy! How are you?*"

Lily had forgotten that Lexi's mum was also Melanie from the hairdresser's. She couldn't stop singing, Myrtle had said so on TV.

"Um," Lily said. "Is Lexi in?"

"She is," Lexi's mum said in her normal voice. And then she was singing again. "*Sorry about the singing! I just can't seem to stop! Hang on a sec, this bottom lock's a bit jammed. Step back a bit . . .*"

Lily and Jimmy took a couple of steps back

while Melanie bashed the bottom door with her hip until it burst open.

"*Come iiiiiiiiiiin!*" She held the last note, arms spread wide. Lily could hear Jimmy snorting with laughter and didn't dare look at him in case she started too.

"That was unexpected," Bug mumbled against Lily's neck. Lily shushed him.

Lexi was in her bedroom, which was at the top of a steep and narrow flight of stairs. Her bedroom was bright and white with a fireplace and a four-poster bed that Lily immediately and desperately envied.

Lexi was sitting on her bed, leaning back against a huge pile of pillows, her tiny, fluffy dog curled up at her feet. "What's up?" she said, as if she had people she didn't know very well turn up at her house every day.

"Um," Lily said, looking at the dog and then at Lexi. "Did you write this?" She held the luggage tag out to Lexi and Lexi grinned, taking it from her.

"Where did you find this?" Lexi asked. Her dog jumped to its feet and stared at Bug. Lily squeezed him gently to remind him of the 'no talking' rule.

"It was in a tree in our road," Lily said. "So it is yours? Esme thought it might be."

Lexi reached out for her dog, pulling her back to sit on her lap. "Yeah. It was sort of a joke. I mean, I would love it if Pom-Pom could talk, but I don't think it's going to happen."

"Pom—" Bug started to say, but Lily squeezed him and he said, "Oof!" instead.

"You're never going to talk to me are you,

Pommy?" Lexi said, her face pressed to the back of her dog's head. "But that's okay, I love you anyway."

Pom-Pom looked over at Lily and Jimmy, her expression mostly vague, but slightly puzzled.

"Thanks for bringing this round," Lexi said.

"Right," Lily said, turning back towards the door. "Er. No problem. See you back at school. When you're . . . better."

"Yeah, it's weird isn't it?" Lexi said. "I can't seem to leave the house when I'm supposed to be going to school. But it's okay, it's nearly Christmas hols."

She held up Pom-Pom's paw and used it to wave goodbye.

* * *

"I thought something would happen," Jimmy said, once they were outside in front of the house again.

"Me too," Lily said. She hadn't really known what. She'd been half-thinking of a crash of thunder or something, but she'd known that was ridiculous. It just seemed like such an anti-climax.

"I told you Grandmother was making it up," she said. "Come on. Let's go home."

"Pom-Pom!" Bug said, shaking with laughter. "That poor dog. No dignity."

"Lily!" Jimmy said.

"What?"

"Look at this!"

Lily turned and saw that Jimmy was crouched down next to Lexi's front step. On the ground was a blue plastic crate full of milk bottles.

"Yeah," Lily said. "Some people still get their milk delivered. Mum says it's too—"

"Not that," Jimmy said. "This!"

He held up one of the bottles. It had a silver top and a Pinewood Dairy label, but stuck to the other side was a luggage tag.

Chapter 11

"*I wish I could be on TV,*" Lily read.

"And that came true for Ms Nutbeam?" Jimmy said.

Lily nodded. "I think so. I don't know why she'd have been on *Pinewood Post* TV otherwise."

"Should we go and see her?" Jimmy asked.

"We need to find the person who made

this wish," Lily said, squinting at the tag. "Not the person it came true for."

"Oh yeah," Jimmy said. "I keep forgetting."

"Who do we know who wants to be on TV?" Lily said.

Jimmy furrowed his brow. "I can't think of anyone."

"Me neither," Lily said. "I guess . . . maybe we go and ask around? I mean, Esme knew it was Lexi's wish straight away."

They walked up the hill towards Poet's Walk, a row of small shops outside of the square. Lily hadn't exactly planned to go there, but she also thought it might be a good idea to avoid their mum's shop, since she didn't think her mum would approve of the two of them trying to match the wishes. She'd had words with Lily last night about not taking Grandmother too seriously, but Lily thought it was worth a try. And her mum didn't need to know.

When Lily was little she'd always gone to Poet's Walk with Grandad. It was near the bungalow he'd lived in when Grandma was alive. They'd go to the newsagent's for Grandad's paper and a comic for Lily, then to Kate's Kakes, where he'd always buy her a cupcake or an egg custard, and then to the pet shop, Woof and Tumble, to play with the kittens. She didn't get to do anything like that with him any more. Not since he'd stopped going outside.

Lily and Jimmy first went into the news-agent's, and showed the owner, Mary, the luggage tag.

"Do you recognise the writing?" Lily asked.

Mary squinted, holding the tag at arm's length. "I don't, love, sorry. Whose is it?"

Lily smiled. "We don't know. That's what we're trying to find out. You don't know anyone who might've wished to be on TV?"

Mary shook her head, handing the tag back to Lily. "I can't imagine anything worse! Poor Myrtle's still not over it."

Mohinder in Woof and Tumble didn't have any ideas either, but he did let Jimmy hold a giant rabbit and got the shop parrot to say, 'Don't make me laugh!' to Lily. Bug rolled his eyes as if talking animals were old news.

116

As they walked into Kate's Kakes and the scent of vanilla and butter hit them, Lily's stomach rumbled.

"Lily!" Kate said from behind the counter. "And Jimmy! How lovely to see you both. And I've just made Christmas cookies, would you like some? They're still warm."

"Yes!" Jimmy said, hopping up and down.

"I'll take one," Bug mumbled.

"No, thank you," Lily said, ignoring them both. "We just wondered if you knew anyone who might have wished to be on TV?" She put the luggage tag down on top of the glass counter.

"Ooh," Kate said. "Are you trying to find who made the wishes? It's all very exciting, isn't it? And a bit spooky." She wiped her hands on her pink and white striped apron and slid the tag closer.

"Well, I didn't know he wanted to be on TV, but I do recognise the handwriting," she said.

"Really?" Lily said.

"It's Arthur. From the roller rink." She tapped the tag. "I recognise the curls on the letters."

"Thank you!" Lily said. "That's really helpful."

"Great!" Kate said. "So do you want some cookies now? On the house?"

"Yes!" Jimmy and Bug said together.

The roller disco took place every Saturday, but Lily hadn't been for ages and Jimmy had never been. His eyes lit up as soon as he and Lily were inside the building.

"Can we skate?" he asked Lily excitedly.

Lily laughed. "You don't know how to skate, do you?"

"No . . ." Jimmy said. "But I could learn!"

"You could," Lily said. "But not today. Today we need to talk to Arthur and see if this is his wish."

"Okay," Jimmy said. "But promise we'll come back!"

"I promise," Lily said. She did actually want to come back. She hadn't been for a while, but standing at the side, listening to the whirr of the skates on the smooth floor and seeing the flashing lights changing the skaters' faces from blue to red to green and back again, made her wish she came more often. It was really fun. She wasn't sure when or why she'd stopped going.

"Is that Arthur in the box?" Jimmy asked, pointing across the room.

"Booth," Lily said. "Yes." The roller disco had its own DJ booth and Arthur prided himself on playing proper old vinyl records rather than digital music. It meant that sometimes the songs skipped or stopped altogether if there was a scratch, but he said it was authentic. Right now he was playing a song about rocking around a Christmas tree.

Lily and Jimmy skirted around the rink, stopping every now and then to watch someone with particularly good moves, but soon they reached the booth and Lily knocked on the door.

Arthur opened it and gestured at the

enormous yellow headphones he was wearing. He held up a finger to signify they should wait just a minute. They watched him lift one record off the double turntable in front of him and put it back into its sleeve and then he said, "What's up?"

"Is this yours?" Lily asked, passing him the luggage tag.

He took it from her and put one large hand up to his face. "Oh! It is, yes! I'm so embarrassed."

"Why?" Lily asked.

"I'm a grown man! Wishing to be on TV . . . Wishing at all. It's silly."

"No, it's not!" Jimmy said. "Why do you want to be on TV?"

Arthur shook his head. "I always have, from when I was a child. I don't think about it much any more, but when I heard about the wish tree I thought, Why not?"

He leaned over and lifted another record out of the box next to the turntables. Lily gasped as she saw what was caught on the corner of it. Another luggage tag.

Chapter 12

By the time school finished for the Christmas holidays, Lily and Jimmy had reunited lots and lots of people with their wishes. They'd found that Sammy in Jimmy's class had wished she didn't have to go to school any more, which explained why Lexi had been stuck at home. They discovered that Hywel from the library had wished his cat would disappear, which explained all of Mrs

Entwistle's cats going missing. He was shamefaced when Lily and Jimmy asked him about it. He said it had been a joke because his cat kept waking him every morning by standing on his face and he'd had enough. He told them if Mrs Entwistle's cats didn't come back, he was going to get her some kittens from the rescue centre.

Every time Lily and Jimmy found another wish, and every time they found someone who'd made a wish, they told their grandad, who noted it in his book. There were still quite a few wishes unaccounted for, but Lily was starting to think maybe they could actually do it – find all the wishes and make everything go back to normal.

They still hadn't heard from their dad, but Mum and Grandmother didn't seem to be worried, saying he could look after himself wherever he was, so Lily tried really hard not to worry too. She wasn't always successful. She couldn't imagine where he could be and was scared he was going to miss Christmas.

"I still don't understand what made all the wishes come true," Jimmy said, while they waited for Mum to get home from work so they could all have dinner together. Grandmother didn't tolerate dinner on their laps in front of the TV. Lily had been annoyed at first, but she'd started to look forward to them all sitting down together.

"It must be the lightning hitting the tree, surely," Lily said. She sat down on the sofa that Grandmother had moved into the dining room from the living room.

"But I thought that's what made them come true wrong?" Jimmy said. "For the wrong people."

"Oh yes," Lily said. "Maybe without the lightning they would have come true properly, you mean?"

"No," Grandmother said. "I think the lightning is the catalyst. It happened the same way before. Without the lightning all you would have is luggage tags on a tree, which I know is what your mayor intended, but it seems wholly pointless to me."

"That's what Lily kept saying!" Jimmy said. "She said it was just like littering, but in a tree."

Grandmother laughed out loud. "Did she?" She looked at Lily. "Don't you believe in wishes?"

"I do," Lily said.

"Now?"

"No. Before. I did, I mean."

Her grandmother looked intrigued. "You've made a wish that came true?"

"I have too!" Jimmy said. "I wished for a bike once and I got a bike. It was Esme's old one, but that didn't matter. I like it."

"That's not the same," Lily said forcefully. "You just asked for that bike."

"What did you wish for, Lily?" Grandmother said.

Lily felt a bit strange. Almost as if her grandmother was hypnotising her. She felt sleepy and floppy and her limbs didn't feel properly attached. She couldn't believe she was about to say it (she'd never said it out loud, not even to Bug) but she could feel the words forming in her mouth, like the boiled sweets Grandad sometimes gave her. She looked at Grandad now for reassurance. He was sorting out the messy drawer, but turned and smiled at Lily. She smiled back, weakly.

"I wished Mum and Dad would split up," she said before she could change her mind.

As soon as the words were out, she felt dizzy.

"Because . . ." Grandmother said gently.

"Because they were fighting all the time. Because they were so unhappy. We were all so unhappy. Jimmy kept getting into bed with me and falling asleep crying and crying and saying 'Mummy' in his sleep . . ."

While Lily had been talking, Jimmy had crossed the room and sat down next to her. Close. His leg and shoulder pressed against hers. He was warm. She realised her other leg was warm too and noticed that Bug had climbed up on the sofa and was snuggled in on her other side. Grandad was leaning back against the kitchen unit and looking at her kindly.

"You wanted to be happy again," he said.

"I didn't even think about that really," Lily said, looking between him and Grandmother. "I just wanted it to stop. And I thought that if Dad left, it would stop. Mum wouldn't be so angry. And sad. I didn't think about Dad being gone. I didn't think about missing him. That Mum would miss him or Jimmy would. I just thought if he wasn't here, they wouldn't be shouting and that would be better."

"But you know they didn't separate because of you," Grandmother said. "It wasn't your fault. It wasn't even your wish. It was just a coincidence."

Lily shook her head. "It was the next day. I made the wish in bed and the following day Mum and Dad sat us down to tell us."

"Doesn't matter," Grandmother said. "Coincidence."

"But how do you know?" Lily said.

"I just do," her grandmother replied.

"Well, that's not good enough!" Lily said. She heard Jimmy (or maybe it was Bug) gasp, but she didn't feel bad about it. Her grandmother had turned up here, telling everyone not to be rational, that of course wishes could come true, but now, as soon as Lily had told her about a wish that had come true, it was just a coincidence?

Lily knew it wasn't. She knew her parents had split up because she wished they would. She knew it was all her fault. And it was probably her fault that her dad was missing too, because if she hadn't made that wish he wouldn't have been living on the canal boat and he probably would be here, at home, with the rest of them. Where he was supposed to be. Where he should always have been.

Chapter 13

"What's the next wish, Lily?" Grandmother asked over dinner the following week. "I wonder how many are left."

"We've just got one tag at the moment," Lily said. "There are no more in the note-book, but there might be more we don't know about."

"What's the one on the tag?" Jimmy asked.

"*I wish I didn't need glasses*," Lily said from memory. "I'm not even sure where to start."

"I think I might know!" her mum said, sitting up so quickly she almost knocked her wine over.

"Really?" Lily said. She frowned. "You believe in the wishes now?"

Her mum picked up her glass and twisted it between her fingers. "I don't know that I believe in them exactly. But there's a little boy . . . He comes in the shop with his gran. I don't know his name, but he's got long blond hair. I thought he was a girl the first time I saw him." She took a sip of her wine. "Anyway, last time they came in the shop, he was talking to his gran about having to wear glasses and he complained about it the whole time. He was very cute."

"But it's grown-up writing," Lily said. "Hang on." She got her jacket, took the tag out of the pocket and handed it to her mum.

Mum shook her head, peering at the tag. "I bet his gran wrote this for him." She handed the tag back to Lily. "She works in the library with Hywel. You could go and see her tomorrow."

Lily thanked her mum then looked at Jimmy who was hopping up and down in his seat with excitement.

"It might not be the last one," Lily told him. "There are probably more."

"I know!" Jimmy said. "It's fun."

"But tomorrow's Christmas Eve," Lily

said. "And if we don't find them all—"

"We will!" Jimmy said. "I bet you. I bet we will."

"Oh yes," said the woman (who turned out to be called Celia), peering at the luggage tag. "I wrote this."

"For your grandson?" Lily asked.

She nodded. "He really doesn't want to have to wear glasses and he really liked the idea of the wish tree, so I wrote this for him and hung it up. Where did you find it? I thought they'd probably all been blown away in the storm."

"They were all over the place," Lily said. "We've found nearly all of them. We think."

Celia went to serve a customer and Lily looked around the library. She'd been going there for as long as she could remember, but she hadn't actually been in for a little while. She'd always loved how grand it was and how it was always quiet.

"It's a bit spooky in here," Jimmy said.

"Hmm," Lily said, looking over at the wall of card catalogues.

"Do you think we need to give the tag to her grandson?" Jimmy said. "Because it was his wish? Or is it okay with her?"

"I don't know," Lily said.

Celia came back and Lily asked when she'd be seeing her grandson next.

"Tomorrow night, actually," she said. "He's coming with me to the tree-lighting ceremony."

"Can you give him the luggage tag then?" Lily asked.

Celia smiled. "I don't think he'll want it. It's a bit grimy . . ."

The tag actually looked charred around the edges, as if it had been burned by the lightning.

"It's just . . . we've been trying to give the tags back to everyone," Lily said, her tummy suddenly flipping with fear that maybe the wishes wouldn't be fixed, and all because Celia didn't want to give the tag back to her grandson.

"Don't worry," Celia said. "I'll give it to him. And will I see you there?"

"Definitely," Lily and Jimmy said together.

As they started to leave, Lily glanced back at the old library card catalogue again. It wasn't used any more as all the books were recorded on computers now, but Hywel kept it because he didn't trust computers. And it was a good job he had because the computers still weren't working, hadn't been since the storm. When she was smaller, Lily had loved riffling through the small drawers full of the cards that were actually (now she thought about it) quite similar to the luggage tags. She walked over for a closer look, pulling Jimmy along with her.

"What is that?" Jimmy asked.

"Card catalogue," Lily said, frowning. "I just . . . thought I saw something."

And then she saw the tag, hanging just slightly out of one of the brass-edged drawers. She reached up and tugged it down. She recognised the handwriting immediately. It was her mum's. And it said, *I wish I could go back to Paris.*

"It was just a bit of fun," Lily's mum said, as Lily dangled the luggage tag in front of her by the white thread.

"You said you didn't believe in wishes," Lily said.

"I don't!" her mum said, catching the tag and pulling it off Lily's finger. "I mean . . . I didn't. I just . . . you asked me what I'd wish for and I started thinking about Paris and then I just . . . It was a bit of fun!"

"Everyone's said that," Jimmy said. "Everyone's said it was a bit of fun! But I don't get what's fun about it if you don't believe the wishes are going to come true, even a little bit."

139

Mum reached over and ruffled Jimmy's hair, then pulled him closer for a kiss that he squirmed away from.

"You're right," she said. "I think everyone probably had a tiny thought, right in the back of their minds, that maybe the wishes might come true."

"And they did," Lily said.

"Is that the last one then?" Grandad asked.

"I think so," Lily said. "Maybe. We've always found the next tag when we matched a wish, so if there was another one, it would be here and I haven't seen any more."

"There's no more wishes in my notebook either," Grandad said. "All the wishes we know about have been matched."

"So now we wait and see what happens at the ceremony," Grandmother said.

* * *

Lily put Bug down at the top of the stairs and he ran straight into her room and jumped up on the bed.

"What if it doesn't work?" Lily asked him, flopping down next to him on the bed, her eyes closed.

She felt Bug's head butting against her arm. "I think it'll work," he said.

"What if Dad doesn't come back?" Lily said, a tear running down the side of her face and tickling her ear.

"He'll come back whatever happens," Bug says. "He loves you too much not to."

Lily screeched as she felt Bug's tongue against her ear. She curled away from him, laughing and rubbing at the side of her face. "That. Was. Disgusting!"

Bug ignored her, turning in a circle ready to settle back down on the bed. And then he stopped.

"Hey," Bug said. "Look at that."

"What?" Lily asked, without moving.

Bug butted his hard head against Lily's side. "Look!"

"Ow!" Lily said. "What?" She sat up, gently pushing Bug away from her. And then she saw what he'd seen. There was a luggage tag on her pinboard. It was crumpled, as if someone had screwed it up and then flattened it out again.

She stood up and crossed the room. Taking a deep breath, she turned the tag over with her finger and butterflies burst in her stomach as she read her own wish. *I wish my dad would come back.*

Lily had got as far as sitting on the end of her bed, still staring at the tag, when there was a tentative knock on her door. The door opened and Jimmy's face appeared.

"Can I come in?"

"You're supposed to be in bed," Lily said.

"I was," Jimmy said, crossing the room and sitting down next to her. "But then I found this under my pillow."

He held out a luggage tag and Lily reached for it, noticing that her fingers were trembling.

Lily had spent enough time helping Jimmy with his homework to recognise his handwriting straight away. He'd written, *I wish my dad would come back.*

"Oh, Jimmy!" Lily said, tears springing to her eyes. She managed to push her own luggage tag into his hand before enveloping him in a hug.

"I was scared he wasn't going to come back because we didn't find it," Jimmy said, his voice muffled by Lily's shoulder. "But he will, won't he?"

"I hope so," Lily said.

Chapter 14

It was finally Christmas Eve. In the town square, the sky was dark and clear, with so many stars twinkling above that it made Lily feel a bit overwhelmed, so she tried to focus on the fairy lights in the trees instead. Carols were playing through the PA system, and Lily could hear people humming along to 'O Come All Ye Faithful'.

Lily and her family sat close to the podium. Bug snoozed on Lily's lap. Jimmy was next to her with their mum next to him. He hadn't been allowed to bring a game with him, so he was squirming in his seat and turning to wave to his friends.

Grandmother was next to Jimmy and, at the end of the row, Grandad. Mum hadn't been at all sure he was ready for something like this. He hadn't been out of the house for such a long time, but he'd wanted to go, particularly since he planned to give his notebook to the mayor to put in the town archive instead of the wishes. He said that as long as he was with his family, he thought that he'd be fine.

Lily thought maybe he would be too.

As the clock on the town hall struck seven, Mayor Smith stepped up onto a small makeshift podium and looked out at the crowd. Rather than the basket of wish tags she'd been holding at the last town meeting, in her hands she had a sapling in a little bag. This time, she only had to clear her throat for a hush to come over the assembled audience.

"I'd like to welcome you all here tonight," she said. "It's so lovely to see so many of you, particularly after the events of the last couple of weeks. We've been through a lot, all of us, but what I love – and have always loved – about this town is that we've all pulled together and supported each other. We're stronger now than we were before the storm, before the tree was destroyed. And now we get to sing carols and eat Christmas cake. Please tell me someone's brought Christmas cake!"

Lily felt someone gently tug on her hair, and she turned to see Esme and her mums slip into the seats behind her.

"We've brought cake!" one of Esme's mums called out.

"And cheese!" her other mum said.

Lily smiled at Esme.

"Is your dad here?" Esme asked.

Lily shook her head and Esme gave her a sad smile.

While Major Smith talked about future plans for the town, Lily spotted Celia sitting next to a little boy with long, blond hair. Celia caught Lily's eye and tapped the little boy, who looked over at Lily and smiled, holding up his luggage tag.

Lily smiled back and felt her own luggage tag in her pocket. She still had no idea if she believed in the wishes, or in what Grandmother had told her would happen if they matched them with their makers, but she and Jimmy had done their best and that was all they could have done.

At the end of her speech, Mayor Smith placed the sapling in a small hole in the ground and tamped the soil down with a spade.

"Merry Christmas!"

Chapter 15

Walking down Elm Avenue towards home, Lily saw him first. Then Jimmy spotted him, and started to run.

"Dad!" Lily yelled.

She heard her mum say, "What?" but Lily was gone, already darting down the street after her brother.

Jimmy was clinging to their dad by the time Lily reached them, so she just flung her arms around them both. Her dad was laughing and ruffling their hair, but almost falling over under the pressure of their hugs.

"Hey!" he said. "It's okay, I'm back now."

"Yes, you are," Grandmother said. "But where on earth have you been?"

"It's good to be back," Lily's dad said, smiling at everyone.

They were all – once again – sitting around the dining table, Bug included. Dad looked rather pale and shaggy and unshaven, and Lily had the usual feeling of not really knowing him very well at all.

Once Mum, Grandmother and Grandad had joined them at the gate, they'd all bustled inside the house. Then, while Lily and Jimmy sat either side of Dad on the big leather sofa, Mum made coffee and Dad explained that he'd woken up in his canal boat in Paris with no idea how he'd got there. Lily hadn't even known there were canals in Paris.

"I can't believe you were in Paris," Lily said. "That was Mum's wish!"

"Was it?" her dad said, smiling at her mum, who was leaning against the counter and picking the nuts out of a box of muesli. "I tried to phone of course, but no calls were getting through."

"The systems have been down ever since the storm," Grandad said, from the other side of the kitchen where he was cutting up some Christmas cake.

"I did send a postcard, but I assume it didn't get here?" Dad said, squeezing Lily against his side and kissing the top of her head.

Lily shook her head and pressed her face into his jumper. He smelled just the same. She was glad.

"How was Paris?" Grandmother asked him.

"I didn't see much of it," Dad said. "I didn't have any money, or even have my passport with me, so I spent most of my time at the British Consulate trying to sort it all out."

"I can't believe you were in Paris," Lily's mum said, shaking her head.

"Me neither," Dad said. "I still don't really understand what happened. But it's good to be back," he said, smiling at everyone.

"I thought something bad had happened to you," Lily said.

"Oh, Lils . . . I'm sorry." Then after a pause, he asked her mum: "Did you think something had happened to me too?"

She shook her head. "I just thought you'd done something selfish and irresponsible."

Lily couldn't help herself. "It's not Dad's fault!" she said.

"It never is," her mum snapped.

Lily's grandmother cleared her throat and said, in a quieter voice than she usually used, "Giles. Louise. You know I love you both." She looked at them and, for a second, almost looked embarrassed. "Well, I hope you know. Because I do. I love you both. But Lily here has been thinking that you two split up because she wished for it to happen."

"Lily!" her mum said.

"I'm not finished," Grandmother said. "That is bad enough. But what's even worse is that she felt the need to make the wish in the first place. She wished for you two to end your marriage because she and Jimmy were so sad having to listen to you fighting."

"Oh, Lils . . ." her dad said. "I had no idea."

"So instead of making excuses and casting blame, perhaps you should be thinking about how you can make your children more secure."

Lily's dad squeezed her and she rested her head against his shoulder. At first she'd been embarrassed and angry when she'd realised what her grandmother had been about to say, but now that it was out, she felt better. She really did. She hadn't been aware of the knot in her stomach until it had gone. She put her hand against the place where she now knew it had been. She breathed in and out. It had definitely gone.

Her mum had sat down at the table and pulled Jimmy onto her knee, but he was trying to wriggle away. Bug was also wriggling on the floor, so Grandmother offered to take him out to 'do his business', as she put it. Grandad said he'd join them.

"I'm so sorry, Lily," her mum said, once they'd gone. "And Jimmy. I had no idea you'd heard us or even knew what was going on."

"You used to be really happy," Lily blurted out. She hadn't been planning to say it. She felt like enough had been said today, but it came out anyway.

156

"We were," her dad said. "You're right. But sometimes things change, and we just weren't happy any more. But we were always happy with you two."

"I just want you to live here again," Lily said. "I want the four of us to be together again. It hasn't been as good since you left."

"I know," Dad said. "I wish your mum and me could make it work, but we've tried and I'm not sure we can."

"Okay," Lily said. And then she frowned. "What did you wish for?"

"I wished I could go back to Paris," her mum said. "You know that."

"No, Dad," Lily said. "What did Dad wish for?"

"Oh," Dad said, pushing one hand back through his hair and glancing at Lily's mum

157

under his fringe. "I wished I could have my family back."

Lily looked at her mum who was opening and closing her mouth without actually saying anything.

"So . . . who did that come true for?" Lily asked, her heart pounding.

"I think . . ." her mum said. "Maybe for me. Or for us."

Lily frowned and then she realised. "Grandmother!"

"Perhaps," her mum said. She looked at Lily's dad and smiled.

"Sorry about that," he said.

Chapter 16

"He's been!" Jimmy said, bursting into Lily's room, holding his Christmas stocking with both hands. "Santa's been!"

Lily sat up in bed and spotted her own stocking hanging from the back of the chair in front of her desk. She swung her legs out of bed and crossed the room to grab it, as Jimmy flopped himself down at the foot of her bed.

"I've been in to Mum and she said to give her five minutes," Jimmy said. "And not to open any presents."

"Okay," Lily said.

"But I opened one already," Jimmy said, pulling open the top of his stocking and showing Lily yet another video game he'd been desperate for.

Lily didn't mind waiting to open her presents. In fact, she'd almost forgotten about presents in all the excitement of Dad being back. She felt so much better now he was home and he'd slept on the sofa last night so he could be with them on Christmas morning. The grabby feeling in her stomach had gone. She didn't feel sick. Or scared.

Last night Grandmother had said she was going home soon, but that she was planning to move back to Pinewood so she could spend more time with Lily and Jimmy. Lily's mum wasn't one hundred per cent convinced that was going to be a successful idea, but she was willing to give it a try.

It would be nice to have Grandmother around more, even though she freaked Lily out a bit. She freaked them all out a bit, but she was interesting and funny too, and Grandad seemed to really like her. Grandmother seemed to have noticed. She'd told them all over dinner the night before that she'd always been a 'man's woman' which had made Lily's mum bite her lip hard.

"Can I open just one more, do you think?" Jimmy asked Lily, peering into his stocking and frowning.

"No!" Lily said. "Wait for Mum. And Grandad. And Grandmother. And—"

Then she had a sudden thought. She turned to look at Bug, who was just getting up from his spot next to her pillow. He looked at her and yawned, stretching with his front paws out and his bum up in the air.

Lily stared back at her dog. She couldn't think when she'd last heard him speak. Had he said anything at bedtime last night? She couldn't remember. Had he even said anything at the ceremony? He'd been asleep on her lap and she remembered putting him down on the ground when she stood up, but had he complained? She didn't think he had.

Her eyes filled with tears. She'd wanted

everything to go back to normal and, yes, sometimes Bug's sarcastic commentary had been a pain, but she hadn't wanted him to stop talking to her altogether, for ever.

"Bug!" she said, moving around the bed so they were almost nose-to-nose. "Can't you talk any more?"

Lily's dog licked her nose, catching a tear that had slipped down one side.

And then he said, "Course I can, you silly sausage."

"It's a beautiful day," Lily's mum said, as Dad joined them to walk up to the square.

"It really is," her dad said.

He'd been back to his canal boat to shower and change and was already looking much better than he had when he first got back.

Lily and Jimmy looked at each other. Jimmy was grinning and hopping up and down, and Lily felt the butterflies back in her stomach, but this time they were nice ones. Once Bug had done his business, Lily saw him look at her parents' linked hands and then at her. You know something's up if even the dog's noticed, she thought.

They didn't talk much as they walked down Elm Street, although Mum and Dad had a good-natured argument about where to go to have their Christmas Day breakfast. Dad said he thought his mum would prefer The Bluebird, but Lily's mum said if Grandmother didn't want to get up in time to join them, she didn't get to dictate where they ate. Then they decided that Grandad could choose, since it was going to be his first meal out of the house for a long time.

Lily thought about how she used to feel sick when they argued before they split up, but how this argument felt different. She felt secure. She checked her stomach for the old hollow, heavy feeling, but it wasn't there.

They paused for a few minutes in front of the *Pinewood Post* where the community TV channel was streaming live. The usual presenter, Jolene Rose, was back and explaining how everything seemed to have gone back to normal. They watched for long enough to learn that Mrs Entwistle's cats had come back, before Jimmy complained that he was starving and so they set off again for breakfast.

They all took the diagonal path across the

middle of the square and when they reached the new tree, Lily stopped to have a look.

It was tiny. It didn't even come up as high as her waist, and the branches weren't even as wide as her fingers, but something about it seemed strong.

And then Lily noticed a luggage tag, tied to the trunk.

As she reached out to turn it over, she realised her hand was shaking.

The tag said, *A new beginning*.

And it was.

Acknowledgements

I had the idea for this book in Disneyland Paris in 2011 and started making notes in Starbucks in Disney Village, so thank you to Walt Disney, I guess. (And to my dad who paid for the trip.)

Thanks as always to my wonderful agent Hannah Sheppard, fabulous editors Naomi Colthurst and Jenny Jacoby, and everyone at Hot Key and Piccadilly for making me feel so welcome. A special mention to Olivia Mead for bone-crushing hugs and 1D love. Huge thanks to Jet Purdie for the gorgeous cover design, Simon Mendez for the beautiful cover art and Dynamo for the lovely inside illustrations.

When I started writing this book, I visited Year 6 at St Francis C of E Primary School and asked the class to write down a wish on a luggage tag. Their wishes were sad and funny and sometimes a bit scary ("*I wish my arch-enemy got stung to death by bees*") but they were hugely helpful in creating Lily's world. So thank you to Aaron Treanor, Abigail Bradley, Asim Hanney, Charlotte Quirk, Chloe King, Daniel Ryden-Vose, Emily Garsden, Ewan Semple, Eve Wilding, Finlay Prendergast, Hannah King,

Harry Lobb, Jacob Maginn, Jenna Taylor, Jordan Parker, Kaya Cooke, Lea Parkington, Megan Hilton, Millie Haworth, Nathan Shaw, Nathaniel Taylor, Niamh Keirnan, Quinn Towler-Hodgson, Robert Marsh, Samera Fareed, Sian Cross, Thomas Kaye, and Tilly Wright-Strong.

As always, I can't thank readers and bloggers enough. Your support, enthusiasm and cheerleading keeps me going when all I want to do is watch *Friends* and read fanfic. This book's a new direction for me – I hope you like it just as much.

Thank you to David for all the things you do. Particularly going out in the rain and coming back with burgers and mulled wine that time. I love you.

This is the first book of mine that my two

amazing boys, Harry and Joe, have been able to read. Thank you for inspiring me, making me laugh, and keeping me motivated with your constant demands to go back to Disneyland. I love you both so much.